For Linda Lou and Lucas

Published in 2006 by The Rosen Publishing Group, Inc.
29 East 21st Street, New York, NY 10010

First Edition

Book Design: Julio Gil

Photo Credits: Cover (boy, wheel) and pp. 5, 15, 22 (wagon) Maura B. McConnell; Cover, pp. 19, 22 (blade, helicopter, rotor) © Tom Nebbia/Corbis; p. 7 © Jose Luis Pelaez, Inc./Corbis; p. 9 © George H. H. Huey/Corbis; p. 11 © Colin Garratt; Milepost 92 1/2/Corbis; p. 13 © Annebicque Bernard/Corbis Sygma; pp. 17, 22 (chain) © Duomo/Corbis; p. 21 © Free Agents Limited/Corbis.

Library of Congress Cataloging-in-Publication Data

Randolph, Joanne.
[Wheels and axles in my world. Spanish & English] Wheels and axles in my world = Ejes y ruedas en mi mundo / Joanne Randolph ; traducción al español, María Cristina Brusca.— 1st ed.
p. cm. — (My world of science)
Includes bibliographical references and index. ISBN 1-4042-3325-3 (library bindings)
1. Simple machines—Juvenile literature. 2. Wheels—Juvenile literature.
3. Axles—Juvenile literature. I. Title.
TJ147.R293 2006
621.8—dc22
2005007738

Manufactured in the United States of America

Wheels and Axles in My World

Ejes y ruedas en mi mundo

Joanne Randolph

Traducción al español: María Cristina Brusca

The Rosen Publishing Group's
PowerKids Press™ & Editorial Buenas Letras™
New York

Contents

Contenido

A wheel and axle is a simple machine. A simple machine makes work easier. A wheel and axle is often used to move something across the ground.

El eje y la rueda forman una máquina simple. Una máquina simple hace el trabajo más fácil. Los ejes y ruedas se usan muy a menudo para mover cosas.

A wheel and axle can also be used like a round lever. This means the axle and wheel move around a fixed point to move an object. A doorknob is this kind of wheel and axle.

El eje y la rueda también pueden funcionar como una palanca redonda. Aquí, el eje y la rueda giran alrededor de un punto fijo para mover un objeto. El tirador de la puerta es un ejemplo de este tipo de eje y rueda.

A wheel is something round. A wheel can be made of rubber. It can also be made of metal or wood. The most important thing is that it is shaped like a circle.

La rueda es un objeto redondo. La rueda puede ser de goma. También puede ser de metal o de madera. Lo más importante es que tiene la forma de un círculo.

An axle is a rod that connects to a wheel. The axle is also fixed to the thing that needs to be moved. An axle can connect two wheels.

El eje es una vara que está conectada a una rueda. El eje también está conectado a las cosas que movemos. Un eje puede conectar a dos ruedas.

axle
eje
HOOK SWL 10 TON

The wheel and axle was first used around 3000 B.C. Today wheels and axles are used in many things. A car uses wheels and axles to move.

La rueda y el eje fueron usados por primera vez alrededor del año 3000 a.C. Hoy, las ruedas y los ejes se usan en muchas cosas. Los automóviles usan ruedas y ejes para moverse.

A wagon uses a wheel and axle, too. Imagine trying to pull your friend along if your wagon did not have wheels. It would be hard to do.

Un vagón también usa ruedas y ejes. Imagínate tratando de arrastrar a un amigo montado en tu vagón. Si el vagón no tuviera ruedas sería un trabajo muy duro.

Radio FLYER

A bike uses wheels and axles. The axle and wheel on a bike is fixed to a chain. A person pedals to move the chain. The chain then turns the wheels and axles.

Las bicicletas usan ruedas y ejes. El eje y la rueda de la bicicleta están conectados a una cadena. Una persona mueve los pedales que mueven la cadena. La cadena hace girar las ruedas y los ejes.

JAMMER
MX SPORT

The rotor on a helicopter is an example of a wheel and axle. The blades are the wheel. The rod that connects to the rest of the helicopter is the axle.

El rotor de un helicóptero es un ejemplo de rueda y eje. Las aspas del helicóptero son la rueda. La vara que las conecta al resto del helicóptero es el eje.

Can you think of wheels and axles you see around you? Look at this picture. Can you find the wheels and axles here?

¿Puedes pensar qué otros ejes y ruedas se ven a tu alrededor? Mira esta foto. ¿Puedes encontrar las ruedas y los ejes?

Blumen Rad

Words to Know
Palabras que debes saber

blade
aspa

chain
cadena

helicopter
helicóptero

rotor
rotor

wagon
vagón

Here are more books to read about wheels and axels:
Otros libros que puedes leer sobre ejes y ruedas:

In English/En inglés
What Does a Wheel Do?
by Jim Pipe
Copper Beach, 2002

In Spanish)/En Español
¡Ruedas!
Step-Into-Reading
by Annie Cobb, Davy Jones. Desirée Márquez (translator)
Random House Books for Young Readers, 2001

Web Sites/En Internet
Due to the changing nature of Internet links, PowerKids Press and Editorial Buenas Letras have developed an online list of Web sites related to the subject of this book. This site is updated regularly. Please use this link to access the list:

www.powerkidslinks.com/mws/whaxles/

Index

Índice

Word Count: 267

Número de palabras: 284

Note to Librarians, Teachers, and Parents

PowerKids Readers are specially designed to help emergent and beginning readers build their skills in reading for information. Sentences are short and simple, employing a basic vocabulary of sight words, simple vocabulary, and basic concepts, as well as new words that describe objects or processes that relate to the topic. Large type, clean design, and stunning photographs corresponding directly to the text all help children to decipher meaning. Features such as a contents page, picture glossary, and index introduce children to the basic elements of a book, which they will encounter in their future reading experiences.